Olly's Treasure

Olly's Treasure

by Elaine Ann Allen
Illustrations by Kelli Nash

Elaine Allen's dedication:

To my own little treasures,
Lindsey and Owen

Once there was a young oyster named Olly, and he loved cleaning the water in the Chesapeake Bay with all of his oyster friends.

But as Olly and his friends filtered the water, Olly could see farther and farther beyond the oyster reef. And he soon spied a sunken ship.

Olly longed to see what was inside the old wreck. "Look," he said to Mr. Oyster, who was sitting beside him. "...a sunken ship. Do you think there is treasure on board?"

"You don't need treasure, little oyster," said Mr. Oyster. "You've got treasure right here, all around you."

Olly looked all around. He saw many oysters, like himself. Some were lined up side-by-side in long rows. Some were sitting on top of each other. And there were other sea animals too, living amongst the oysters. But Olly couldn't see treasure anywhere.

Suddenly, Olly felt very restless. He broke free from his place on the oyster reef and headed for the old sunken ship.

But before he got very far, Mrs. Skillet Fish stopped him.

"Where are you going, little oyster?" asked Mrs. Skillet Fish.

"I'm going to find treasure," said Olly.

"Oh, how interesting," said Mrs. Skillet Fish. "Will you bring me back a gold coin? I need a clean surface to lie on for my bed."

"I'll do my best," said Olly. And he continued on his way to the old sunken ship.

But before Olly got very far, Mr. Mud Crab stopped him. "Where are you going, little oyster?" asked Mr. Mud Crab.

"I'm going to find treasure," said Olly.

"Oh, very fine," said Mr. Mud Crab. "Will you bring me back a silver vase? I am very small, and I need a place to hide from predators."

"I'll do my best," said Olly. And he continued on his way to the old sunken ship.

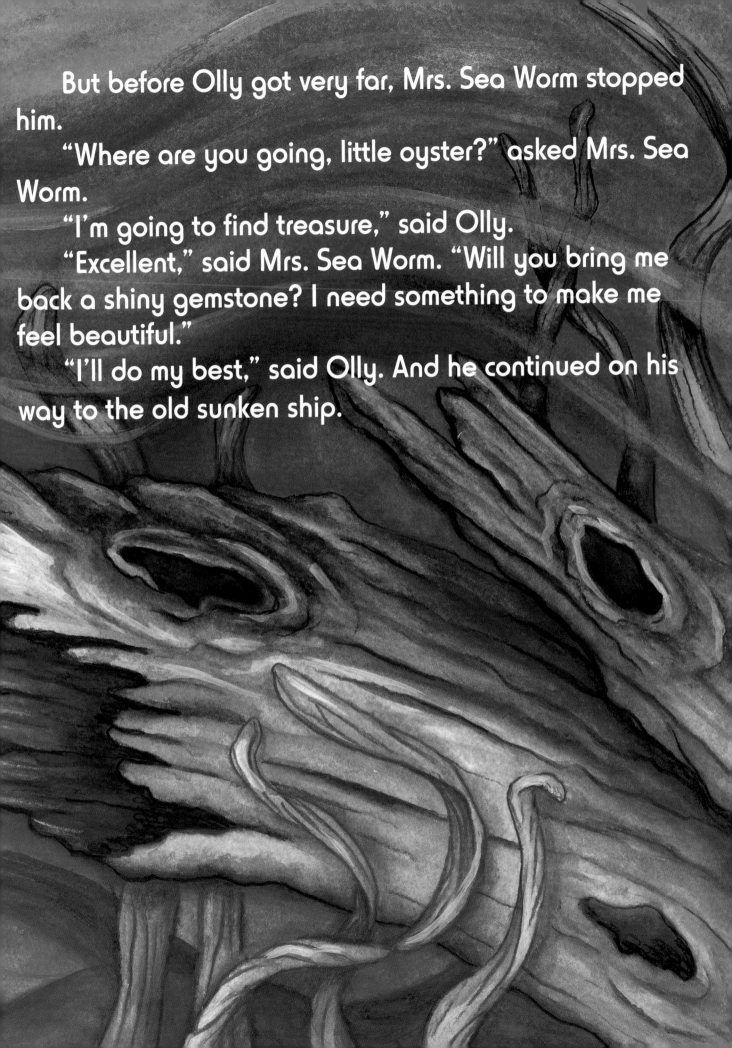

But before Olly got very far, Mrs. Sea Worm stopped him.

"Where are you going, little oyster?" asked Mrs. Sea Worm.

"I'm going to find treasure," said Olly.

"Excellent," said Mrs. Sea Worm. "Will you bring me back a shiny gemstone? I need something to make me feel beautiful."

"I'll do my best," said Olly. And he continued on his way to the old sunken ship.

Olly traveled for the rest of the day before he finally arrived at the old wreck. As night began to fall, Olly used the last rays of sunshine to light his way. He meandered through dark shadows, sagging doorways, and broken wreckage.

And, finally, there it was before him. More
treasure than he could have ever imagined.
There were gold coins, silver vases and
shiny gemstones everywhere he looked in
the bottom of the old sunken ship. He settled
down on a pile of jewels and fell asleep.

When Olly awoke the next morning, he was very cold and very lonely. He looked all around. There were no oysters lined up side-by-side, or on top of each other. There were no other sea animals either, like Mrs. Skillet Fish, or Mr. Mud Crab, or Mrs. Sea Worm. And there was no one to share the treasure.

Suddenly, Olly felt very restless. He quickly found his way out of the old ship and headed for home.

Soon Olly reached the oyster reef. But, he realized that he had forgotten to bring back gifts for his friends. He had been in such a hurry to return home that he had forgotten.

When Olly came to Mrs. Skillet Fish, he told her, "I am sorry Mrs. Skillet Fish. I have returned from my journey, but I have nothing for you."

"Quite alright, little oyster," said Mrs. Skillet Fish. "I don't need a gold coin. I have a clean surface to lie on right here on the oyster reef. And she snuggled down on top of a friendly oyster for a mid-morning nap.

When Olly came to Mr. Mud Crab, he told him, "I am sorry Mr. Mud Crab. I have returned from my journey, but I have nothing for you."

"That's okay, little oyster," said Mr. Mud Crab. "I don't need a silver vase. I have a place to hide from predators, right here on the oyster reef. And he crawled underneath a friendly oyster where he had found shelter.

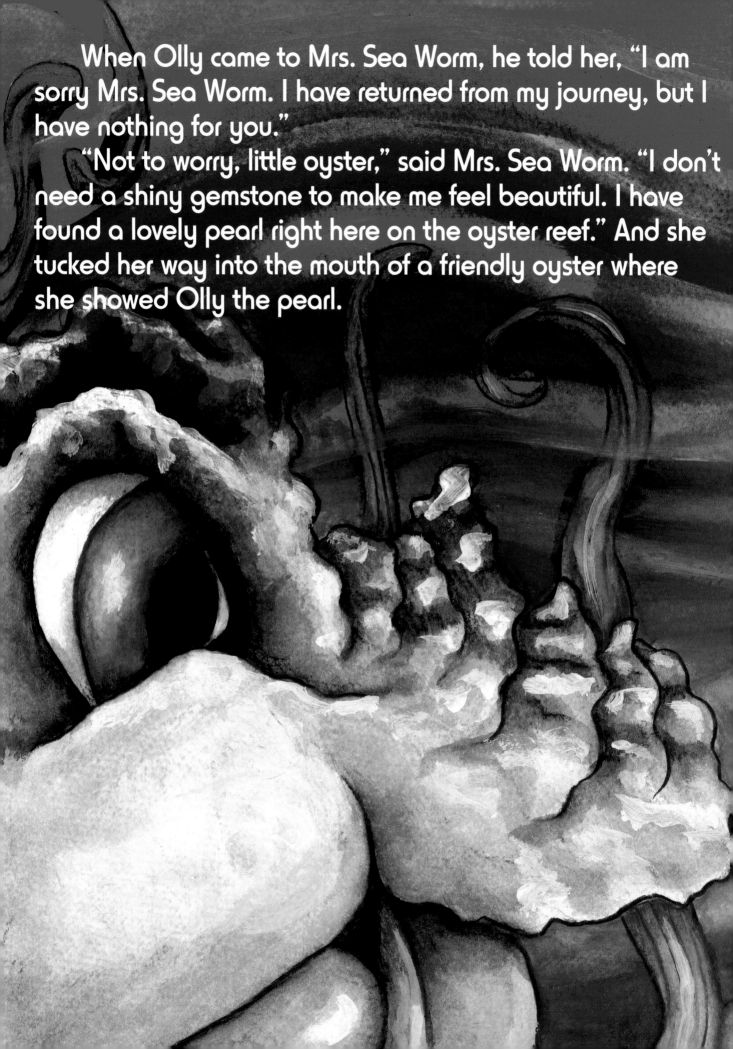

When Olly came to Mrs. Sea Worm, he told her, "I am sorry Mrs. Sea Worm. I have returned from my journey, but I have nothing for you."

"Not to worry, little oyster," said Mrs. Sea Worm. "I don't need a shiny gemstone to make me feel beautiful. I have found a lovely pearl right here on the oyster reef." And she tucked her way into the mouth of a friendly oyster where she showed Olly the pearl.

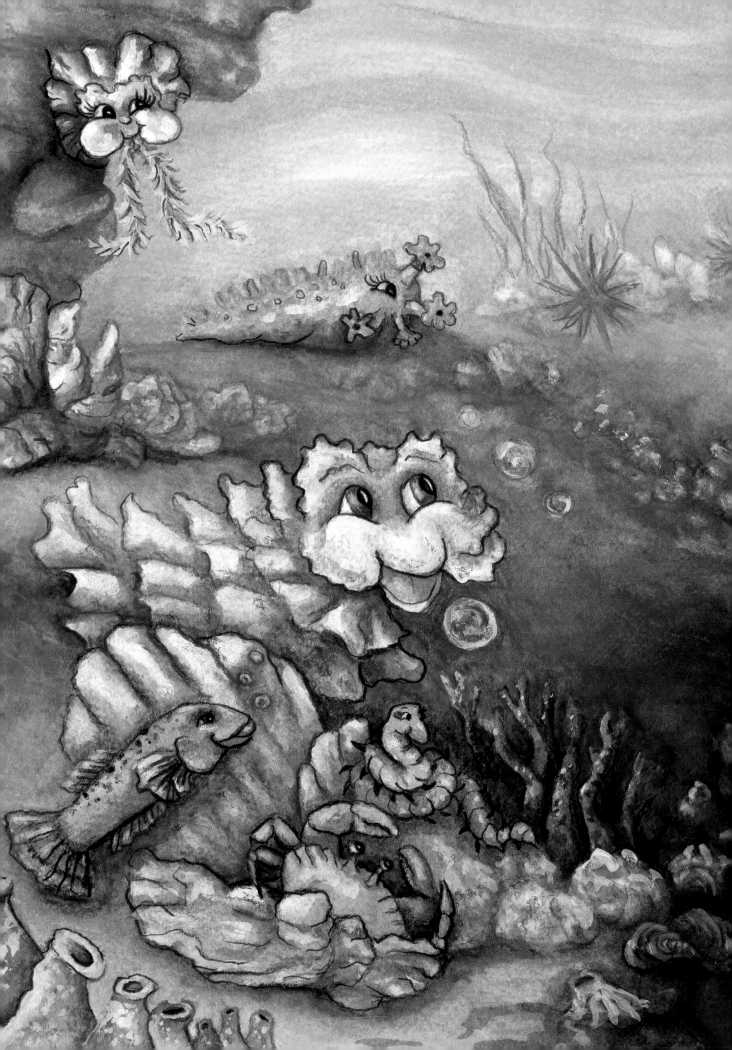

Soon Olly reached his own special place on the oyster reef. He looked at the long rows of his oyster friends who were sitting side-by-side and on top of each other. And he saw all of his sea animal friends nestled in and around the oysters. It felt good to be home.

"Did you find treasure?" asked Mr. Oyster who was sitting beside him.

"Yes!" cried Olly happily. He had found treasure. It was all around him. Right here on the oyster reef.

Olly the Oyster Cleans the Bay. Elaine Ann Allen Illustrated by Kelli Nash. An oyster wanted to settle down with a minnow fish friend to help clean their habitat, the Chesapeake Bay. Learn how they succeeded. Preschool to grade 2.

Size: 7" x 10"	15 color illustrations	30 pp.
ISBN: 978-0-87033-603-4	hard cover	$13.95

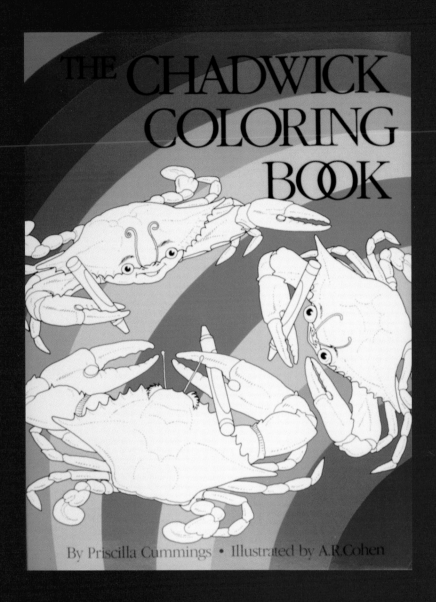

The Chadwick Coloring Book. Priscillia Cummings. Illustrated by A.R. Cohen. Meet a blue crab and other creatures that inhabit a shady creek. This coloring book teaches about aquatic life. Preschool to grade 2.

Size: 9" x 12"	33 b/w illustrations	32 pp.
ISBN: 978-0-87033-389-7	soft cover	$3.95

Another Schiffer Book By The Author:

Olly the Oyster Cleans the Bay, ISBN: 978-0-87033-603-4, $13.95

Type set in Horatio BT

ISBN: 978-0-7643-3772-7
Printed in China

Schiffer Books are available at special discounts for bulk purchases for sales promotions or premiums. Special editions, including personalized covers, corporate imprints, and excerpts can be created in large quantities for special needs. For more information contact the publisher:

Published by Schiffer Publishing Ltd.
4880 Lower Valley Road
Atglen, PA 19310
Phone: (610) 593-1777; Fax: (610) 593-2002
E-mail: Info@schifferbooks.com

For the largest selection of fine reference books on this and related subjects, please visit our web site
at
www.schifferbooks.com
We are always looking for people to write books on new and related subjects. If you have an idea for a book please contact us at the above address.

This book may be purchased from the publisher.
Include $5.00 for shipping.
Please try your bookstore first.
You may write for a free catalog.

In Europe, Schiffer books are distributed by
Bushwood Books
6 Marksbury Ave.
Kew Gardens
Surrey TW9 4JF England
Phone: 44 (0) 20 8392 8585; Fax: 44 (0) 20 8392 9876
E-mail: info@bushwoodbooks.co.uk
Website: www.bushwoodbooks.co.uk